Along Came You

Written by
Karona Drummond

Illustrated by
Estelle Corke

ZONDERkidz

ZONDERVAN.com/
AUTHORTRACKER
follow your favorite authors

Along Came You
Copyright © 2009 by Karona Drummond
Illustrations © 2009 by Estelle Corke

Requests for information should be addressed to:
Zonderkidz, *Grand Rapids, Michigan 49530*

Library of Congress Cataloging-in-Publication Data: Applied for
ISBN: 978-0-310-71508-5

Drummond, Karona, 1965-
Along came you / written by Karona Drummond ; illustrated by Estelle Corke.
    p. cm.
    Summary: Through simple, rhythmic text, a parent tells a child about how life has
been changed, and enhanced, since the child was born.
    ISBN: 978-0-310-71508-5 (jacketed hardcover) [1. Parent and child--Fiction.] I.
Corke, Estelle, ill. II. Title.
PZ7.D826Alo 2009
[E]--dc22

                                                            2007040472

Editor: Bruce Nuffer
Art direction & design: Merit Alderink

Printed in China

09 10 11 12 • 6 5 4 3 2 1

Children are a gift from the Lord.
-Psalm 127:3

Before you,
    my home was decorated in style.

After you,
    my home is decorated in love.

Before you,
   my world was quiet.
After you,
   there is joyful noise.

Before you,
    I ate my oatmeal alone.
After you,
    there are always guests for breakfast.

Before you,

I liked to watch the rain.

After you,

I like to dance in the rain.

Before you,
I liked to dress up.

After you,

I like to dress up.

Before you,
    I traveled light.
After you,
    every outing is a big event.

Before you,
    eating out included candlelight and soft music.
After you,
    eating out includes art and entertainment.

Before you, the biggest thrill at the amusement park
was riding the roller coaster.
After you, the biggest thrill is seeing your face
when you are finally tall enough to ride.

Before you,
  I read books with a thousand pages.
After you,
  I read your favorite book a thousand times.

Before you,
   I slept soundly all night long.
After you,
   I wake to watch you sleeping.

Before you,
        I was me.
After you,
        I am still me. But you are with me.
Life became amazing...

after you.